Ladybird, Ladybird
Ruth Brown

Andersen Press · London

Ladybird, Ladybird, fly away home,
Your house is on fire, your children are gone.

Ladybird, Ladybird, blown by the breeze,
Over the cornfields, and over the trees.

Ladybird, Ladybird, lands in some smoke.
There's really a fire; it wasn't a joke.

Ladybird, Ladybird, fly away, fly.
That frog has a hungry look in his eye.

Ladybird, Ladybird, which way to go?
The old snail is friendly, but he doesn't know.

Ladybird, Ladybird, please do not pause
Close to those dangerous, razor-sharp claws.

Ladybird, Ladybird, pass the pig by.
He's too full to think: too lazy to try.

Ladybird, Ladybird, go to the crow.
Ask him the way home, he'll probably know.

Ladybird, Ladybird, lost in the wood.
Squirrel can't help, though she wishes she could.

Ladybird, Ladybird, will she be blown
Further away from her children and home?

Ladybird, Ladybird, help is at hand.
The bees will show you the lie of the land.

Ladybird, Ladybird, all's clear at last.
Fly to your children, fly home to them fast.

Ladybird, Ladybird, safely back home.
It isn't on fire, and your children aren't gone.

They are all sound asleep, snug in their nest.
Now you can join them; at last you can rest.